DIGGING DEEP DOWN IN THOSE ROOTS

Poetry of Black Hair, Culture, Resilience, Personal & Collective Trauma

Katina Horton

Illinois

DIGGING DEEP DOWN IN THOSE ROOTS,

Jacket Cover design by Katina Horton

Jacket Cover photograph by Jody Lynn Photography

Jacket Cover Image – Adobe stock image

Printed in the United States of America

https://thevalleyofgrace.com

ISBN: 978-0-578920-59-7 (hardcover)

This book is dedicated to all the warrior women who have pledged to do the courageous work of digging deep down in the cultural roots of their hair, themselves, their families, their communities, their nation, and their ancestors.

"Once you had no identity as a people; now you are God's people. Once you received no mercy; now you have received God's mercy."

1 Peter 2:10, NLT.

Contents

Humanity's Quilt

Everybody has a story.

But

It's not

About us.

Only

Reflecting back

To him His glory.

Our stories

reveal the pain,

The hardships,

The trauma,

The mountains,

The valleys,

And all its drama.

Our stories

Give us our square,

Our patch

of material

on the quilt,

As we sit

Adjacent to

All the other squares

Representing

Stories from all over

The world.

One gigantic quilt of love,

Sewn together by

Humanity.

My Colored Umbrella

Yes,

I choose

To be molded,

Softened,

Hardened and

Reconfigured

In all the right places,

With all the right faces.

To reconcile

The hurt

And pain,

And the colored umbrella

That protects us from the rain.

The umbrella of

Character, culture,

Justice, integrity,

And peace.

The umbrella fought

For

So hardily

By our ancestors,

The deceased.

The umbrella that shouts out,

"Go deeper into self-love.

It is there that you will learn

To give out the love that others

Needed."

The umbrella that has told us:

There is no respect of persons.

Everyone is welcome

to gain respite from the rain."

You MUST go through.

Reach into empathy.

And sit THERE

in the other person of color's pain,

Under their colored umbrella.

The Body

The Body,

Is it clean?

Has it been taught

It's been bought,

And then sold

And left for auctioneers.

And my family

To behold?

Placed in chains.

And emotionally drained.

Then placed on a boat.

Headed to the place of the unknown.

The place that will

Forever

Be called,

"The stripping away of

Humility.

The place

That will be called,

"God is here.

Even in the chains."

God is here.

Even in the clauses.

God is here.

Even when equality

Means you're not a whole person.

He has always

Granted to you wholeness.

The freedom

That exists

Outside the physical realm.

Sister of dark melanin.

Your body is part of

His Body-

The Body of Christ.

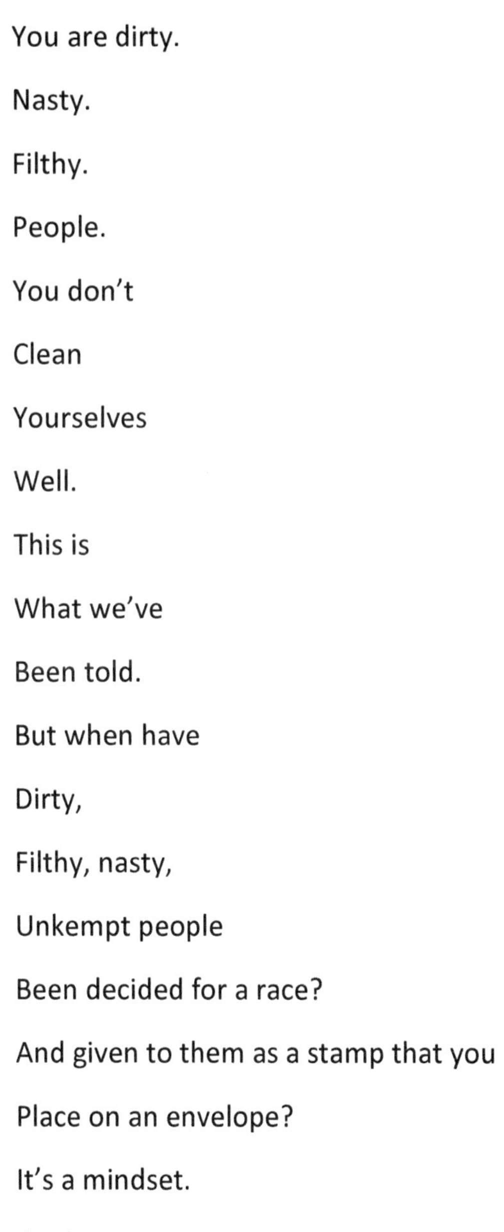

Clean

You are dirty.

Nasty.

Filthy.

People.

You don't

Clean

Yourselves

Well.

This is

What we've

Been told.

But when have

Dirty,

Filthy, nasty,

Unkempt people

Been decided for a race?

And given to them as a stamp that you

Place on an envelope?

It's a mindset.

A misnomer.

Passed down from generation to generation
To make us think that we
Are not humans.
Dehumanized.
Uncivilized.
For the
Simple
Truth
Of the fact
Is...
Any person of any
Race
Or ethnic
Group of
People
Could
Leave the labels
Upon them.
But to keep the power to yourselves,
In your psyche.
Your intellect.

The one must become

The

ALL.

Wear These Tights!

Wear these tights!

The ones that are made specifically

For us, by us.

Wear them on

Your black and brown

Skin, till they

Make you flinch,

Throw up, cower

Within.

"I'm supposed

To focus on

My blackness,

Dancing,

the gift that

God has given me.

Instead, focus has shifted

To wearing these tights.

the ones that manifest

the unspoken:

we are the default,

we have the power.

we are in charge of

hindering

you, this hour.

your expression.

sent to regression,

as you are told,

"Wear these tights!"

The Ebonics Train

Ebonics

Is what we call it.

It’s language.

Filled with expression,

Love,

Culture,

Struggle.

It’s the vowels

And consonants

Doing their own thing.

Walking their own walk,

dancing

In the darkness of

Injustice.

The language of freedom.

our own language.

Where rules are

Made up

As you go along.

Where the

Expression of black

Takes on a pattern

Of its own.

It's Ebonics.

That's what we call it.

The Black Table

All the black kids
Sit at the table.
At the black lunch table.

What they talkin' 'bout?
Talkin' 'bout what Big Momma cooked
Last night.
How the family danced all night,
Grooved all night long,
How they Grooved and Swayed,
And Boogied on down.
Down to the flo'.

While Big Momma fried up
Them chicken wings and pork chops.

No code-switching
at the black table.
Just 'xchanging bits of information
Among our own folk,

Among our kings and queens.

Hydrant Life

I got my spider web
French-braid hairstyle
This mornin'.
Peastew did it.
I can't believe I
Get to look like this,
So pretty.
And wouldn't ya know,
That Madea pressed my hair
Fo' days ago.
Yep, that's right.
But, guess what?
I went outside in that
Hydrant water.
Yep, the kids on the project block
Turned on the hydrant,
Letting the water run loose,
Hoping that the Po Pos didn't come
And turn it off.
'Cause there's no pools for black

Folk to be dippin' in.

We were told that we

Pollute the pool.

"Who said that?"

"I don't know.

Me and you both

Know it ain't cool."

Black Superwoman

Hold those tears in

Don't cry!

Wipe your eyes!

No time for that.

You are a black woman.

Superwoman.

Super strong.

Showing those Emotions

Makes it all go so wrong.

The problem with this logic

Is that it stems from the

Wrong base.

It was given to

Our people at the

Auctioning block race.

We can be strong.

Be super.

Be vulnerable.

Be all those things.

Be in charge of the nation.

Have a room

In the

West Wing.

But our people must learn

To release

The emotions.

The trauma

That has begged us

"hold it in"

Like our momma.

To shed the stigma

That blacks

Don't cry.

Don't break.

Don't release.

What's within.

Release the lie.

Release the dye.

Release the Superwoman

That's been pinned.

Wash Those Dishes

"Get up here!

Wash those dishes!"

"We better hurry

'fore Madea

Come down here

And blast us

With those switches."

"Add the water.

Then the soap.

Then pour plenty

Of that bleach."

"Till the smell reaches

Our lungs,

Becomes more like a leech."

They comin'

I'm washing down the walls.

Our cousins from down South are coming on in.

Tho' our cousins not just

Our Cousins.

They more like

bonded friends.

Lil Willie's Ride

Did you know that Lil Willie

Bought a ride that's so sweet?

He den

Spent all

his lil cash

So he can

Model

Down the street.

Mrs. Guy

Yesterday,

I bought a sour pickle

From Mrs. Guy.

Had to go back down there,

And my mother asked why.

Forget my insert.

You know?

The one that's full of dye.

Momma, you know what I'm talking 'bout.

Talking 'bout the thick peppermint stick

That you place in the middle.

Till the salt and the sweet

has you dancing

with a fiddle.

You know you black

You're black.

Your dignity

And integrity,

Self-respect

Not kept intact.

Because

you see,

Your skin

Erases

all those things.

And all we see is lack.

Not complaining.

'Motionally draining,

And with my service

I give back.

So, wash, and rinse,

And dry again.

And just absorb

Those facts.

Crying Is a Luxury

Cry.

Just cry.

Just let it all out.

You see crying is a luxury,

From when slavery came about.

Hold it in.

Just suppress.

Don't you say a mumblin'

Word.

To your wife

Or your kids

As we gather them like herds.

Black folk don't do therapy.

Black folk don't do therapy.

We pray and we cry.

Yep, we cry in private.

But in public our tears run dry.

Black folk don't do therapy.

We're strong as a people.

We just slay in the Spirit.

Till our Prayers hit the steeple.

Black folk don't do therapy.

We just hope and we pray.

That our unhealed

Brokenness

Will up and leave us some day.

Black folk don't do therapy.

'Cause we think it's a sin

If we bring down from

bondage

Generations had to win.

Black folk must do therapy.
'Cause then we can negate,
Ev'ry game that's been
Played
'Gainst the enemy
Called hate.

Black folk must do therapy.
Till we break all devices
That's been sewn
Into seeds.
Then planted
With preciseness.

Black folk must do therapy.
So our kids
Will one day see,
That our growth,
Faith, and healing

Was a bicycle

Made For me.

My Hair is Nappy

My hair is nappy and kinky.

Don’t you see the bee-bee shots

In the back?

I don’t look pretty.

Look crazy and silly.

Matter fact, these

‘tails look whack.

Your hair is beauty.

It’s my creation.

Your hair, the glory

Part of me.

You queen from Africa.

Queen from Sonship.

Queen from My Identity.

From the Low End

I'm a black woman

From the low end.

It's what they call it.

A section of town,

You know,

Down in the 30's and 40's.

For all those folk,

That's painted brown.

On the south side

Of Chi-town.

'Cause God granted me

The wisdom, knowledge,

direction to walk

Through

Oppression-driven strife.

I've walked through

Everythin' down

On the Low-End

Called the workplace.

Ageism, Sexism,

Racism, too many

"isms."

To be told the truth.

I'm a black woman

From the low end.

It's what they call it.

A section of town,

You know,

Down in the 30's and 40's.

For all those folk,

All those women,

All those black folk

painted brown.

The Real Truth

We can't put someone

Like you on display.

You'll look supreme,

Degreed, and professional.

'Can't have this

'Mong our race.

And in case you forget:

You from the Low-End

The very low-End.

'Better leave

Fo' you catch a case.

Your Hair Not Good Enough

You have to straighten your hair.

You can't come in here

Looking like that.

No weave.

No extensions.

No Braids.

No twists.

This is the workplace.

This is our list.

Privilege conversation

"I don't like the word privilege.

I worked hard.

My family was poor."

Privilege means a 400-year start.

'Fore I even hit the door.

Head start on luxury, savings,

Education, even mo'.

Buying houses, gaining stocks,

Fighting modern day slavery

On all the butcher blocks.

Privilege is a luxury.

'Tis an in-born

Racial thing.

Not getting what's deserved.

Awaiting a ride upon

That swing.

The swing is the ladder.

The ladder is the system.

The system has already been set.

Go to school.

Obey the rules.

No matter how hard

You work,

You will never be

Next.

Think privilege.

Good Hair

You have good hair,

Filled with waves

You comb for days.

Slap on some water.

And oil.

And go.

I have bad hair.

My hair is thick.

Thick and Gummy.

No Length or Even Sequential,

Like Playing a Game

Of Rummy.

Popping

We know that we shouldn't

Be popping.

And rocking.

Rolling these tummies.

Being like the fast girls

Playing gin rummy.

The Guys at the Pool Hall

The guys at the pool hall.

Smoking their cigarettes.

Looking cool.

With their Kangol hats,

And those

Long, gold chains

Hangin' on their necks.

Bringing those styles

From Africa,

The Motherland.

Into the Streets

Of Chi-Town.

Broken Hair Dreams

I felt good about

Getting my hair pressed

Until

I started sweating it out.

It drew back.

Then the other

Black seventh-grade girls

Made me the

Laughingstock.

Look at her!

Look at her!

The back of

Her hair

Has

Bee-bee shots.

Cracker Jack Box in the Sky

We moved into this

Cracker Jack box.

‘Partment so tight

Can’t cuss out a cat.

But we love this place.

This spot on the South side.

This spot where it’s rough.

Yes, we love this place.

‘Long as they

Don’t break in here

No mo’,

And steal all our stuff.

Eye Doctor Blues

I hate going to the eye doctor.

They dilate.

And dilate.

Till I think I got a belly ache.

After while,

I can't read

What's on that screen

Anyway.

Asking me to read

The letter I see on the

Lowest line.

Then, they done given me

This eye patch.

Like it's a gift or something.

"Welcome to first grade!"

I hate going to the eye doctor.

Same Process

I oiled my hair today.

Yep, I oiled

My hair and scalp.

You know how it is

For black folk hair.

Oil it every three days.

Then roll it up.

Makin' sure I put

Tissue on those foam

Rollers.

Might not have any hair

Fo' it's all over.

What Y’all doing?

What y’all doing in there?

Just playing paper dolls.

Y’all better not be lying.

I can see you in the hall.

What y’all doing out there?

We ‘bout to play “It”.

Y’all better not be lying.

I see you doing all those splits.

What y’all doing out there?

Just talking to our friends.

Friends bet’ not start with “m”

And end with letter “n”.

Freedom of the Hair or the Migrants?

I like to part my hair

Experiment, ya know?

Do I want French braids

In the front?

And twists in the back?

Or vice versa.

'Lencia let me experiment

On her hair.

When I was a young'un.

Parting that hair.

Separating the sections with

Rubber bands,

And then French braiding

Each piece of hair,

Then each row.

Making streets and lanes

Going places

I had never gon' befo'.

Places like the Great Migrants,

You know.

Those who left

the South

Looking fo’ freedom.

Instead, they got

Some freedom

Alright.

Freedom looked like racism

Wrapped up in

A box.

With a nice, red bow.

Promised Land

Don’t feel like
Combing my hair
Today.
‘Cause I’m tender-headed.
Tender-headed black folk
Cry when they comb
Their hair.
Sometimes, thinkin’
‘bout it puts a
Weariness in your soul.
But you know,
We keep pushin’
‘Cause we want freedom.
Pullin’ and Pullin’
Each section of hair.
‘Til we enter the Promised
Land.
The land of freedom.
Flowing with grease.
And parts.

And beauty.

Like Dr. King.

And John Lewis.

And all the other black folk

Who marched with them

When there was weariness

In their souls.

But they pulled,

And pulled

With their speeches.

Till they pulled the

Unknown strength

And motivation

Out of the people.

'Til they got up and marched.

Marchin' was their 'xpression

Of Freedom.

Freedom to the Promised

Land.

Their Business

Grown folks don't like it
When you ask them about their business.
"Where are you going?"
"Going to see a man about a dog."
"How old are you?"
"Girl, don't you know you never ask a grown woman
'bout their age,
Or their nation?"
I guess
That's the
End of that conversation.

That Thang Called Grief

Looting, rage, protesting
In the streets.
When we sit right down
And think,
They're all forms of that
Thang called grief.
It grabs you in the chest,
Makes the wise act
So wild.
It chokes in to the reserved,
Makes them look just like
A child.
It's name is grief
Yeah, I said it.
And you better be careful
While you judging'.
'Fore it come up behind you.
And and blind you.
Give your insides
Quite a nudging'.

Waitin' to Eat

I'm sitting at this counter here.
Waiting to be served
like everyone else.
But I'm not everyone else,
is what they say.
They have degraded my rank
and status.
'Cause my melanin got in the way.
I'm just as worthy
as the rest of y'all.
Waiting to eat
my food and be served.
There's no way these tired feet are
Getting up.
Yep.
I'm staying right here.
Black folk tired.
Ti'ed of being passed over at the lunch counter.
That's why I'm waiting
Right here.
I'm sitting at this counter here.
Waiting to be served like everyone else.

African Beat

We knew we'd overcome.
Walked a mile in the Mississippi sun.
Just keep marching to that
African beat.

We hummed for days.
And sang for nights.
Got back home.
Looked such a sight.
Just keep on marching to that
African beat.

We interlocked our precious hands.
Marched way cross Selma to freedom's land.
Just keep on marching to that
African beat.

But God saw us in our pain.

We were herded.

Places in chains.

On ships and boats

That held our reins.

But God saw us in our pain.

We were lynched.

Dehumanized.

As our cries reached heaven's skies.

But God saw us in our pain.

We were hosed.

We were clubbed.

We were whipped.

And we were scrubbed.

But God saw us in our pain.

We were lied on.

Stumped and pried on.

Voting rights?

Had Them denied on.

But God saw us in our pain.

Naming Scheme

Like hairstyles,

Black folks have all kinds of unique

Names.

Yolanda, Shoquonda,

Rolanda, Shonda.

Refusing to be like the caste system

Times-

Black folk took those slavery

names

And did away

With them.

Gave their kids a new name.

A name reflecting the Motherland

Of Motherlands.

A name reflecting freedom.

Nothing like the old.

Like Daddy did with Jacob.
Gave him Israel instead.
Black folks walk around
In the streets,
Shouting out,
"There go Bo-Peep."
"Look at Lil Willie".
"I thought I saw
Greasy Hands the other
day."

Other folk don't understand
That kind of love.
The love that
Goes with black
Folk picking
A name.

The love that started back in
Slavery times

When black folks

Had nothing.

they could call

Their own.

Like our Daddy,

Calling us his own,

When others think

We need to be their

Property.

Daddy says,

we're his.

Daddy says our Names are

Written on the palms

Of his hands.

Can the church

Do call-response?

Can the church just

Say

Amen?

The Mouse

I came home from school.

Walked in the

Bathroom.

And looked

In the tub.

To my shock,

There was a mouse.

Makin' the tub

His little hub.

Fell straight through

The hole in

The ceiling

Where the

Men were working on

The plumbing

Problem.

What do I do now?

Close the door.

And wait.

Wait for momma

To come home.

Out of sight,

Out of mind.

But not really.

I wish Fluffy,

Madea's cat,

Was here.

She'd know what to do.

But Madea needs

Fluffy

'Cause she has a lot of friends, too.

So, I sit and wait

For momma to

Come home.

With the door

Closed.

In my own

Little hub.

In the living room.

Pastor on the Pew

When the pastor
Gets happy,
He starts walkin'
Cross the pew.
The first pew.
I wonder if they leave that
Pew open
'Specifically
For Him.
As he walks across in his robe,
Sweating, humming,
hooping, holl'in,
"In the morning,
In the morning,
Everything gonna be
Alright.
In the morning."
I think Pastor
Thinks he's David.
That he can run over

Troops and leap

Over walls.

'Stead of walls,

He's leaping over

Pews.

Today I'm making cornrows in my hair

Today, I'm making cornrows in my
Hair.
Better be careful though.
I don't want the rows
to be pulled
too tight on the ends.
I'll be having bumps for days.
Right back there
In the kitchen.
Bumps.
and pulling.
and headaches.
For days.

The other day I made flat twist cornrows.
I did a good job.

Two days from now, I will be adding
Some grease 'tween those rows.
So, my hair won't dry out.

But today,
I'm making cornrows in my
Hair.

The Heart of Worship

I love me some mornin' worship.
Deacons get so happy
when we start to sing
During
the call to worship.
Hearts of black folk get so happy.
I tell you,
You'd think we were back
In the Motherland.
'Stead we're here.
On the south side of Chicago.
In Our own Wilderness.
God sees us through.
Been guiding us with a fire by night,
And a cloud by day.
As we face every day
Problems black folks face
in the black community.

The Hair Wait

Today
I'm going to the shop.
I'll probably be there
Fo', five
Hours.
Yeah, that's right.
You heard me.
More like Five, six actually.
Black women
be sitting 'round
with magazines.
Some without.
Tryin' to figure out
What they want done to their hair.
Kids and babies will be hollerin'.
And screaming.
Women will be coming in
Twisting their curves and figures,
Hoping black male beauticians
Will see what they've been
Blessed with.
And then bump them up
On the hair waiting list.
Everybody
And their momma
Will be at the black beauty shop.

Climbing the Mountain

On my way home
from the Meat Market.
Probably have to walk up eight flights
Of stairs.
Elevator probably won't be working.
Tryin' not to think about it.
Can't help it.
Five flights of stairs
Carryin' five bags.
Lawd, have mercy on my soul,
As I climb this mountain.
The mountain of stairs.
And the mountain of injustice black folk been climbing
for years.
Maybe when I get to the top
I'll see a transfiguration
Like Jesus did when he hung out
With Peter, James, and John posse.
Maybe the transfiguration will be inside of me,
New vision and such.
Maybe Once I reach the top,
the top of the stairs,
I'll be holler' out like Dr, King,
"I have seen the Promised Land!"

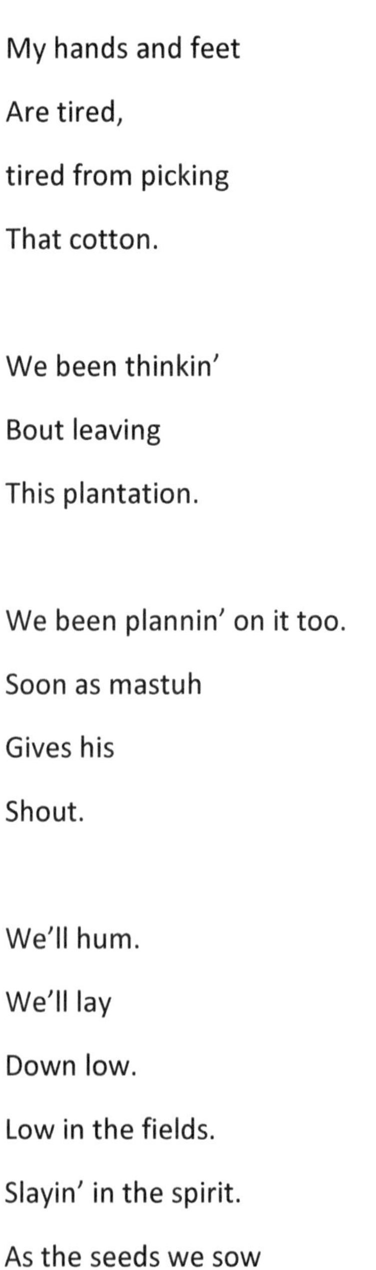

Planning Our Escape

My hands and feet

Are tired,

tired from picking

That cotton.

We been thinkin'

Bout leaving

This plantation.

We been plannin' on it too.

Soon as mastuh

Gives his

Shout.

We'll hum.

We'll lay

Down low.

Low in the fields.

Slayin' in the spirit.

As the seeds we sow

Are planted.

And the route

We take are granted.

As our God

Has Moses lead

Us to Underground's

Most pearly gates.

Hairology

Why yo' hair this way?
I braid my hair.
So, you can stare.
Y'all don't know?
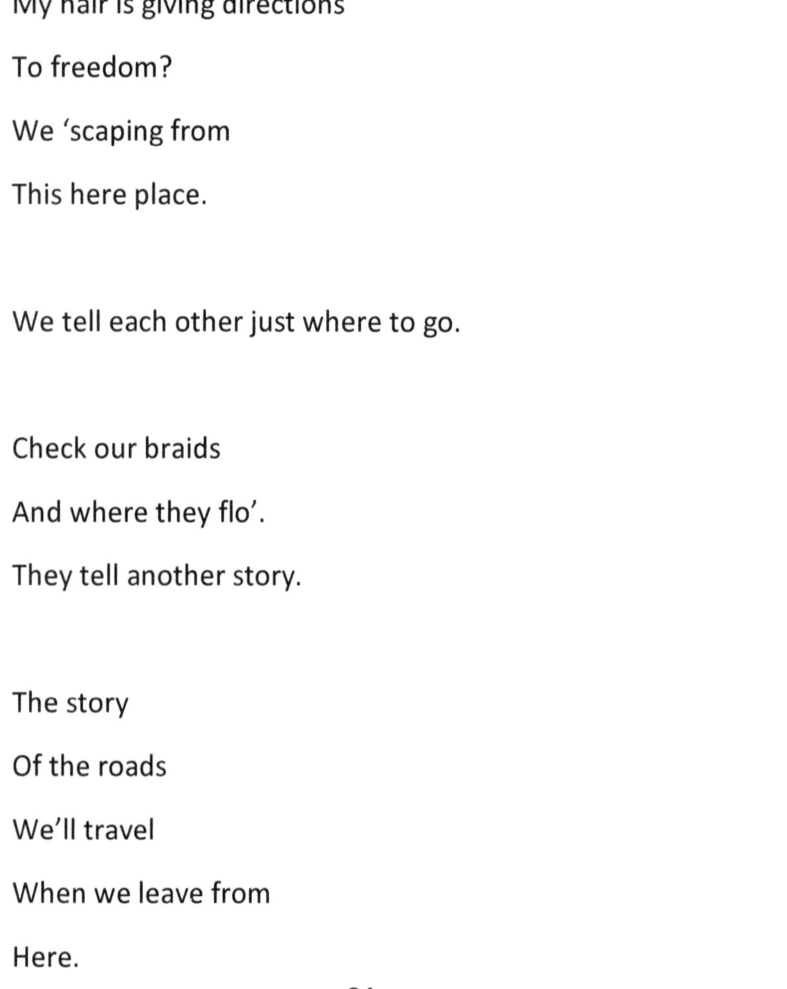
My hair is giving directions
To freedom?
We 'scaping from
This here place.

We tell each other just where to go.

Check our braids
And where they flo'.
They tell another story.

The story
Of the roads
We'll travel
When we leave from
Here.

Leavin’ with God’s great grace.

We waitin’.

Waitin’

On God to mediate.

Beauty Shop Struggle

As I'm sitting in the beauty shop,
There is
Temptation.
A burning desire.
To up and
Leave.
Been sitting here fo'
Three hours already.
Just plain tired.
Worn out.
I think they forgot
About me.

Next thing I know,
I hear the shampoo
Guy call my name.

Time to get
my hair shampooed.
Time to get my

Midnight ‘do.

Blue Magic

They say that Blue Magic
Is like magic.
'Cause it helps the
Straightening comb
Do it's thang.
Helps that comb
Sizzle and drizzle and make
Your hair so slick and straight.
It's like magic.
Blue magic.
And it's hot and running through
Our whole entire race.

Argo Starch Hype

I went to the meat
Market
For lottery tickets, cigarettes, and Argo starch.
Black folks in the hood
Love them some starch.
We chew it often.
Like it's the best thing on earth.
I think we got that from the grown folk.
Who chew Argo Starch
Like their feet touching Southern dirt.

To Perm or Not to Perm

I wanted a perm.
Not sure
That was the best thing.
My hair
Started coming out in patches.
My hair is thick.
But Super strength lye
Was too much for my hair.
I wanted a perm.
Not sure
That was the best thing.
Cause
My hair
Started coming out in patches.

They travelin'

They travelin' from near and far.

Black folk

Multiplying the numbers in the North, East, And

West.

They travelin' by train

Looking their Sunday best.

In dresses and suits

And patent leather boots.

Headed for freedom.

They call it Migration.

The Ninety-Nine

We say black lives matter, or do they really?

Do we think that God cares about all his children?

Even the one that was held down for nine?

Or, do we think that he's just fine,

Just happy, so happy with only

The Ninety-nine?

Itchin' Hands

I heard grandma say that her
Hand is itchin.
Folk from the south say that when they
Waiting for money to come their way.
They also say things like,
"The Lawd will make a way."
When they are down to their last dime
And nothing but
Margarine in
The 'frigerator.
God always showed up.
He showed up for
Us folk.
Like when we laid out on the mourners'
Bench calling for him all night.
Taking pray
Without ceasing to a whole
'Nother level.

Reenacting the Church Scene

Fo' some reason,
Black folk
Love re-enacting
The church scene
At home.
Think it's like balm to their souls or
Something.
Somebody gotta be preachin'.
Hooping
And hollerin'
Someone else gotta be
The deacon.
Then you need the ushers
Collecting money
And seating someone.
Then you need
The choir in the robes,
Singing and swaying 'til
The spirit
Come upon folk.
Giving praise God a whole
New meaning.
Fo' some reason,
Black folk
Love re-enacting
The church scene
At home.

AT the County Hospital

I have to go to the doctor today.
But I don't feel like it.
The doctors are good.
Don't get me wrong.
But I have to wait so long.
It's the public hospital.
Best doctors in the world.
But I have to wait so long.
Could have picked some greens,
Baked a turkey
Made some sweet potato pies,
Pressed some hair,
All kind of things.
'Stead, I'm spending
My time in the
Waiting room.
At the county hospital.
Where else will the poor folks go?
Somewhere that you have to
Wait too long.

Jheri Curl

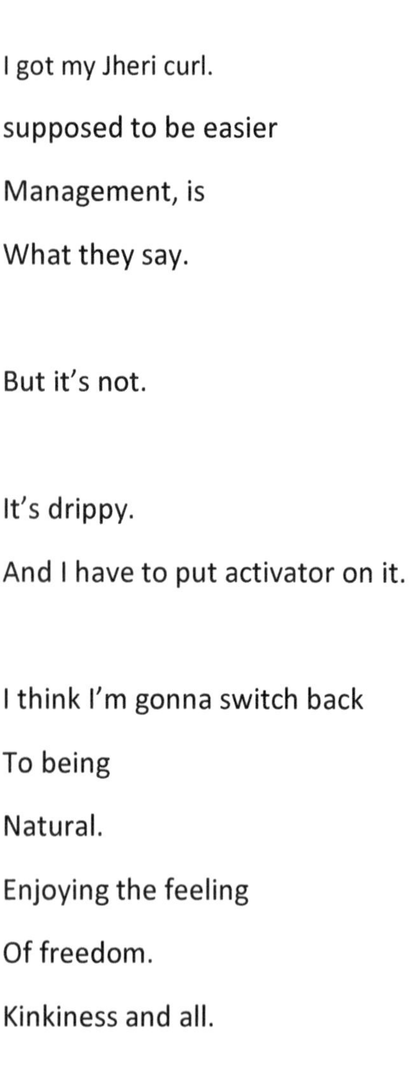

I got my Jheri curl.

supposed to be easier

Management, is

What they say.

But it's not.

It's drippy.

And I have to put activator on it.

I think I'm gonna switch back

To being

Natural.

Enjoying the feeling

Of freedom.

Kinkiness and all.

What seemed like less work

Became more bondage

in the end.

Popping and Sizzling

Not sure if I want to help cook.
What I wanna do is watch.
And admire.
And eat
When the food is ready.
I wanna
watch Madea make
The long strips for the chicken and dumplings.
I want to watch her place the strips in the
Grease.
as the popping and the sizzling
Makes the
music of its own.
I wanna experience
Madea cooking.
Makin music of her own in the kitchen.
Creatin'
her own rhythms and such.
Moving to the beat of her own inner drum.

The Everlasting Arm

Love you,
Is what she said
'Fore Abba came and got her
To lay down her head.
Sufferin' was over.
But we sho' gone miss
This pillar.
What we gone lean on
now for support?
Abba,
The Everlasting Arm.

How Santa Claus Looked in the Ghetto

Peastew loved jammin' to James Brown
On Christmas Eve.
Singin' strong.
Hoping fo'
All the kids in the ghetto
To get a toy
on Christmas morn.
And somehow,
it all worked out.
Po' black folk
found a way to bring those gifts in.
Make the kids
Feel special.
Make the kids feel loved.
Mo' importantly,
The love of the
Father.
Focusing on baby Jesus in the manger.
the one gift
Fo' Christmas
All folk
Needed.

In the projects,
Kids shared their toys with one another
On Christmas morning
Anyways.

Peastew loved jammin' to James Brown
On Christmas Eve.
Singin' strong.

Hoping fo’
All the kids in the ghetto
To get a toy
on Christmas morn.
And somehow,
it all worked out.

I’m Flying Like An Eagle

I made it home.
I’m what they call
A latchkey kid.
Don’t bother
Me though.
‘Cause while
Momma’s still
At work,
I’m having my own
Party.
Called a one-woman
Party. Got my
Momma’s
Record player
going.
I’m *flying like an Eagle*.
Yes, to the Sea baby.
That’s the name of the Song.
I’m *sitting in*
The park, baby.
Dancing and Feeling
Free.
Till the phone rings.
And momma’s
Checkin’
To make sure
I’m doing my homework.

“Yes, Momma.”
Now, Why
Did I go an lie?

Didn't want her
To know
I was with the eagle.
Way high, up In the sky.
Meaning in her stuff.
Meaning big trouble.
I put the music
Back on
When I get off the phone.
I'm with the eagle again.
Grooving.
Swaying.
Making history.

Almost time for Momma
To come home.
I put everything
Back in place.
"Good girl mode."
No need to disturb the order of perfection.
The order of perfection
For the black human race.

We must keep
The records lined up
Like gold.
The ones that have kept us
Grounded in the trials
And the madness
We behold.

better
Get my homework
Done.
Or else

My bottom will
Be like gold
As well.

As the pretty as the Rest

I'm stitchin' this here
Dress out of
Canvas
And tater sacks.
You gon'
Look as pretty
As the rest of
These girls.
Your hair silky,
Pressed.
and your bobby
Socks
And mary janes too.
You go on, and play now.
I'm gon' fix ya' up
Real nice.

Love you She Said 2.0

Love you
Is what
She said
When she
Had little
Left in
Her and
'fore God
Took Her
up
To the
Sky.
Love you
Is what
She said
When her
Tears
Were running
Dry.
Love you
Is what
She said
When she
Could not
Serve any
Longer.
"God Is
Taking me
Home, Girrrl.
This pain
You ache
Make you

Stronger."
Love you
Is what
She said
Last words
She Said
to me.
They will
Be kept
In my
Heart.
They'll be
Kept in
My Blackness
Sea.

Our Hair Shows

We must
Create as a person
As a people.
As a race.
Till it reflects
In churches'
Steeples.
Our hair
Is a
Monument.
A pyramid
Of creating.
Displaying
The artistry of emotions.
The mountains.
The valleys.
the peaks.
The lakes.
the rivers.
the seas.
Our hair gives the story
Of our story.
Our slavery song.
Of Jim Crow laws.
Our hair shows
The Civil Rights
Movement and the
Funkiness of
The 70s.
The Empowered
Fro's.

Our hair shows
Our need to assimilate
Into the work
Place culture.
No need to upset anyone
Who takes on the role
Of a vulture.
Our Hair shows
Our struggles with
Identity.
It's within Our Hair.
His glory.
As we wiped our perfumes
On his feet with
Our fro's
In a dance
Of worship.
Then he
Rested on day seven.
Our hair shows.

Black Love.

Black man.
Black woman.
Black Love.
Love you baby.
Love you babe.
Is what they say.
They hug.
Black man protects.
Black women nourishes.
He remembers
The rules of walking with
Black woman
On the street.
He walks
On the street side.
Black man protects.
Black woman nourishes.
They hug.
Black man.
Black woman.
Black love.

My people like to go.

My people like to go.
They like to go dancing.
Dancing and wearing
Their finest,
Their Bostonians.
And Stacy Adams.
And pin-striped suits.
And patent leather
Mary Jane shoes.
Black purses.
Their Sunday best.
Our people.
My people.
They like to go.
They like to go dancing.
Dancing and wearing
Their finest.

The Many Facets of Black Hair

Artistry of black hair.

Wavy, straight,

Wiggy, gummy, kinky, nappy,

Natural, sew-ins,

Throw-ins.

It's black hair.

Silky, shiny, locky, twisty.

Cornrowed, twist outs, Sweat out.

It's black hair.

Those Plats

Ms. Sable wants me to pick up

Sweet potatoes

From the grocery store.

On the way there,

I see Bobby Jones.

I like Bobby,

But I didn't want him to

See me like this.

Momma shampooed my hair

Last night.

Today,

Madea is gonna press it.

But right now,

I got plats in my hair.

Members of the Great Migration

Folks in the South leaving paychecks.

Selling off everything that they own, so

they can hop on the train to freedom.

They don't know what's in store for them.

But they gotta go.

They gotta do something different.

Definitely don't want

To be thought of

As looking crazy.

Playing cards.

Grown folks love playing cards.

All kind of cards is what they say.

They shuffle, and then shuffle some more.

Us kids better not be caught playing cards.

We show gon' be in some trouble.

'Cause if us kids are caught,

Then we committing a sin.

It's okay for the grown folk.

When grown folk play cards

They talk about grown folk things.

Us kids have to go in the back room.

Not in the front.

And then pretend like we not listenin'

To the conversation that goes on

As

Grown folks play cards.

Sister Coleman

Me and Willie saw Sister Coleman.

She fell out.

Yes, she did.

She fell out.

slain in the spirit.

Mother board say she got happy.

Willie and I were laughing silly

till

One day I caught what Sister Coleman had.

We never laughed again.

How Black Folks Doin'

Ever ask a black person how they doin'?

Their response:

"Well, I got up this

Mornin'.

I got 'tivity of my limbs.

I can put one foot in front of the other.

I guess if they can move then that means they alright.

Tho' after getting' a lickin'

From Big Momma,

I don't think I am.

The Jacks Girls

When girls play jacks,

They know they gotta be quick.

Their eyes gotta be quick.

Their ears gotta be quick.

Their hands gotta be quick.

One slip of the finger

And you don’ lost the whole game.

Maybe that’s why there’s a love

And hate relationship between me

And jacks.

The Corner Store

I went down to the

Corner store.

Everybody and their momma

Were in there.

Lines were wrapped around the aisles and back.

What's everybody buying?

salt pork, spam, pound of this, pound of that.

Lottery tickets,

Cigarettes, Argo starch.

I think some folks just in there to see

Everybody and their momma.

Sitting on the Bus

Seems like we been
Sitting here
At this
Bus station
Forever.
Sitting and waiting.
They say
The bus to Memphis is
Running late.
It's always running late.
Should've
Brought a book,
So I could meditate
On God and his goodness.
And thank him for the fact
That I can sit anywhere I want
On the bus now.
Anywhere.
No going to the back.
Though there's a lot

More problems

Us black folk

Still having.

Though where we sit on the

Bus isn't one of them.

Crazy Morning

I told him to put the casserole
In the oven.
I got home.
Ain't nothin' been done.
What I'm gonna do now?

"Oh, momma,
I overslept.
That's why nothing
Is in the oven."

I better start praying
Jesus keep me near the cross.
Or near somethin'.
I can't believe folk
Getting ready
To come over here
And ain't nothin' ready.

What Happened to Grandma's Hands?

Did I tell you about the miracle

Of grandma's hands?

Arthritis got a hold of 'em.

Then Ms. Mable down the street

Held on to them

Like she was holding on for dear life.

She started holdin' and prayin'.

And prayin' and holdin'.

And God moved on Grandma's hands.

He moved till something got hold of her.

And then when folk asked Grandma

How she was feeling, she said,

"I can pray.

Cook.

And sew.

And clean.

God is good.

And I'm alright."

Far away in a dream.

We need

Hope, and we sing.

Hope,

And we live.

Hope,

When hope seems

Far away

In a dream.

We sing

Hope, and we glean

Hope.

When hope seems

Far away in a dream.

We shout hope.

We pout hope.

When hope seems

Far away

In a dream.

Fast and Mannish

They tell the girls

Not

To be

Fast.

And the boys

Not

To be

Mannish.

What's fast?

Acting older

And liking

Boys.

What's mannish?

Acting like

You a grown man

And smelling yourself.

Different Shades

Black folk come in all different shades.

That's right.

All different shades.

Of brown.

And black.

Yellowish-brown.

Caramel.

Light-brown.

Medium-brown.

Dark-brown.

Coffee-bean brown.

Then black.

Dark-black.

Medium-black.

And glistening blue-black.

We are a mixture of moods

And shades.

Same creator.

When God painted us

He made us

Part of his masterpiece.

He played with

Colors in the

Warm zone.

Hard for us to feel

It though.

Been pressed down for so long.

Lil Willie

"Hey, I know you.

Ain't you Big Mable's

Grandbaby?

I've known you

Since you

Were a little baby.

How your

Momma doin'?"

"Fine."

"Okay, girl.

Tell Big Mable

I said hi.

Tell your momma

I said hi.

And when you do,

Tell them it

Was Lil'

Willie, Big Willie's son.

Okay?"

"Okay."

My Masks

Today, I left out
For work.
Putting on my masks.
The mask
Of code switching.
Hair straightening.
happy all the time,
Suppressing emotions
Mask.
When I get home,
I take off the masks.
I can use Ebonics,
Or any other words
For that matter.
Wear
Kinky, nappy,
Hair.
And process my
Anger without
Being thought

Of as the angry,

Black woman

Because of

Injustice.

And yell.

And scream.

To El-Roi,

My God,

The God who sees

Me in

My oppression.

Walk on Gold

We wear the gold.

The gold of the kings

And queens from the Motherland.

From the Land of Africa

Where our ancestors journeyed.

One day we will

Not have to

Wear the gold.

We will walk

On the streets

Of gold.

The gold

That

Was

From

Our

Father's

Land.

From

God

Our

Father.

The

Land

That flows

With

Milk and honey.

Praise Dance

When I praise dance,

I worship God.

I bow down

To him

With my

Alabaster box.

My offerings to the Lord.

I used to carry all

My pain

And oppression

In this box.

The dance

Helped me to

Release it.

The praise

Helped

Me to see

It.

Trade in my pain

For the

anointing of the Lord.

Deep Hurt

When you
Watch black movies,
You see the same thing.
The real.
At least
For the ones
That show
The black folk
Running and
Screaming
And hollerin'
And screamin'.
Look like
They losing their
Minds.
They not.
They just getting it out.

'tween them and the

Lord

In their own way.

Been held in so long

As a people.

400 years

type of long.

Black Church Happenings

When black folk black church,

They know

They gone be there all

Day long.

'Cause there's gonna be

worshippin'.

Shouting.

Singing.

Preaching.

Dancing.

and more

Worshippin'.

Shouting.

Singing.

Preaching.

Dancing.

Then the call to the altar,

Where Pastor

Gon' ask

Black folk

If they want to

Be delivered.

Delivered from what?

Their sins and hell.

The Proverbs

Madea had

All the proverbs.

The meanings didn't

Reveal themselves

Till

Adulthood hit.

Then I couldn't

Help myself.

At work.

At play.

With my kids.

Wherever I went,

I could

Hear her voice.

Following me.

Imparting her

Words of wisdom.

Imparting her

Ancestors'

Wisdom.

Imparting our God's

Wisdom.

Little pinch of this.

Madea made everything
from scratch.
Little pinches of this.
And little pinches of that.
A little dash of this.
and a
Little dash of that.
Never put too much
Of this.
And never put too much
Of that.
Little pinch of
This made
Four-layer cakes.
Little pinch of that
Made gumbo and stew.
Never put too much
made
Buttermilk
Cornbread.

The lunchroom cookies.

All the black kids

Knew about

The lunchroom cookies.

The Peanut butter Cookies.

And the Butter cookies.

You had one cookie,

And you thought you'd died and gone to cookie

Heaven.

Surely,

Nothing tastes as good

As these.

Funny how the

Brain never lets

You forget

Certain things.

Like the 10 cent cookies

That we ate in the

Lunchroom.

We were poor.

But eating them

Made you feel rich.

Special.

'Cause

All the black kids

Knew about

The lunchroom cookies.

Momma's Instructions

"Make sure you lotion your skin.

Put Vaseline on your lips.

No ashy 'bows."

These are Momma's instructions

Before I leave the house.

Forbid if I look like I'm not

Being taken care of.

Madea and the Currency

Heading to the Currency Exchange.

Five-block walk.

Not far.

But we gotta take

Care of her business.

At least that's

What the

Grown folks say

When they don't want

Kids asking them

About what

They're doing.

This time,

I'm her cane.

Next time,

It will be another

Granddaughter.

Gotta make sure

I do my job well.

I let her

Hands rest
On my tiny little
Shoulders,
As I'm
Upholding
The pillar of the
The community.
Of the North
Brought from the
South.
That was
Birthed
Out of
The caste of
The slavery system.

The Dream

The dream of a
child in the projects.
The dream of being
Doctors and lawyers.
And teachers
And preachers.
The dream
Of being singers.
And dreamers.
And authors.
And thinkers.
The dreams that formed
In the Renaissance Era and
Traveled in the form of
Zoot suits and pocket
Watches.
Poet laureates.
And excellent
Speakers.
The dreams.

The dreamers.

The messages.

The gleaners.

Simplicity

My grandmother

Was a

Simple woman.

But

Even in simplicity

You have

Things that

You like.

Make you feel

Good about

Yourself.

seen.

known.

Hers

Was polishing

Her fingernails.

Colors of all

Shades.

Sometimes

One coat on top

Of the other

If she was out of remover.

But

She'd polish them.

Admire them.

They were her

Work of art.

And she smiled.

And admired her

Fingernails.

The simplicity

Of having

Her nails

Done.

Making her feel

Like a Queen

Straight from the Nile.

His Birthday

Every year

On Martin Luther King's

Birthday,

We had an assembly at school.

What I remember most is

Jamming

To Stevie Wonder's

Song.

His Happy Birthday song.

Singing and swaying

With our kind.

With our people.

Our ancestors.

God's steeple.

When the Words Were Gone

The slaves sang
when their words
were gone.
When they
were taken
captive
all in a
night's wrong.
But they kept
Singing.
Like
Hannah
When she
Prayed
And prayed
For that baby
Until Samuel
Was born.
They sang and
They sang.

Till their

"Moses"

Showed up.

And their words

Weren't gone.

'Cause all they could

Do was to sing their new song

"We's free"!

And then we were told

We were placed in chains.

And then we were told

You are free.

We went way cross Maine.

And then we were told

You are free.

We traveled South.

And then we were told

You are free.

Did many things

To suppress our mouths.

And then we were told

You are free.

Resilience

It's resilience.

brilliance

built within.

Our failures.

Our sins.

Our kickdowns

and all arounds.

Getting back up once

we have been pinned.

Pinned down on the mat.

The mat of injustice, oppression,

desertion, obsession,

homelessness, and trauma,

and poverty, and drama.

resilience.

Brilliance

built within.

healing.

adaptation.

It is ours, my friend.

Beef and Brandy

We're going to beef and brandy.
Waiting for the lunchtime special.
Patty melt and fries.
Not sure how long it's going to take
us to get there.
Momma seems to be caught up in
Carson's.
Next it will be Field's.
Smelling
And telling.
And telling and
Smelling,
Every perfume that
Exists behind the
Make up counter.
It's going to
Be a long day.
But I will make it.
I have to.
I'm

Waiting for the lunchtime special

At Beef n' Brandy.

The patty melt and French fries.

the forty acres and a mule

Kind of waiting.

7 Eleven

7-Eleven is only three blocks away.

Feels like 20 in this Memphis sun.

I am for sure

That death has

Taken hold

Of our face.

Our bare feet.

Our melanin

In general.

7-Eleven is only three blocks away.

Feels like 20 in this Memphis sun.

And that is all I have to say.

Forgot the Key

I took the Cottage Grove bus home.

It is below zero outside.

How far below

I can't recall.

All I know is that my toes

Are starting to sting

In these below zero boots.

I rang the bell.

No answer.

I don't have my key.

What will I do?

Walk to my uncle's house.

Only been there a few times.

I hope and pray that I remember

Where he lives.

I hope and pray

That my feet will

Be alive.

I took the Cottage Grove bus home.

It is below zero outside.

How far below

I can’t recall.

All I know is that my toes

Are starting to sting

In these below zero boots.

The Kinds of Hair

Black women make up
All kinds of hairstyles to express
Themselves.
Frenchbraids, plats, and twists,
Connected to ponytails
And buns.
Connected to
Frenchbraids, plats, and twists,
Connected to ponytails.
And buns.
This poem could go on forever.
Kind of like the artistry
That's going on in my head
Right now.

I’m gonna keep on eating

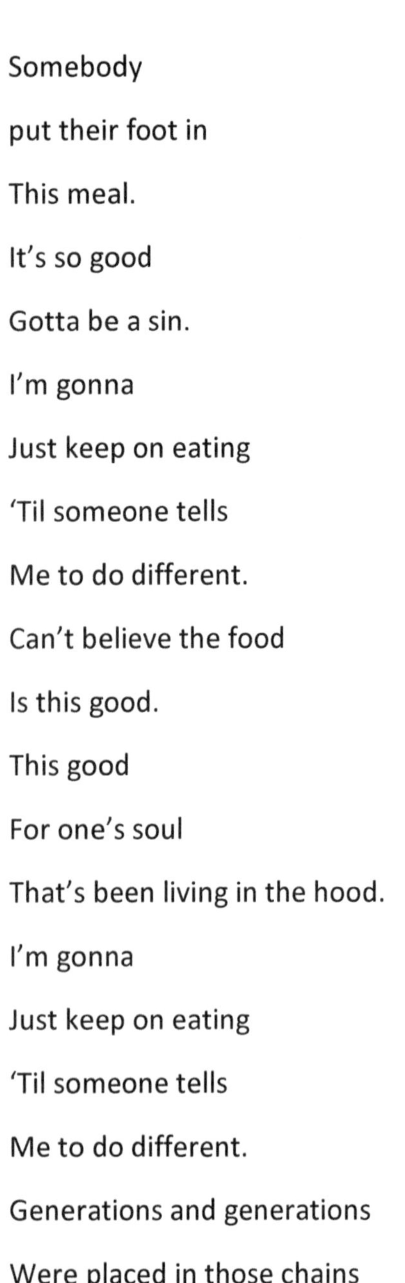

Somebody

put their foot in

This meal.

It’s so good

Gotta be a sin.

I’m gonna

Just keep on eating

‘Til someone tells

Me to do different.

Can’t believe the food

Is this good.

This good

For one’s soul

That’s been living in the hood.

I’m gonna

Just keep on eating

‘Til someone tells

Me to do different.

Generations and generations

Were placed in those chains

By the time we were free,

Some folks definitely were insane.

I'm gonna

Just keep on eating

'Til someone tells

Me to do different.

The Bud Billiken

Headed to the Bud Billiken
Day parade
With Peastew.
It's going to
Be wild.
And fun.
And all kinds of crazy.
But we will see the parade.
And when it's over, we will see all the
Black folks like us
Setting out blankets.
Foldable chairs, and tables.
Barbecue grills.
Ready to get their eat on.
Whole park
Will be full of them.
Expressing themselves
On the grill.
And listening to music.
Jamming to the O'Jays or

The Isley Brothers.

It's going to

Be wild.

And fun.

And all kinds of crazy.

But we will see the parade.

And when it's over, we will see all the

Black folks like us

Ready to get their eat on.

No trick or treating

Momma said

No trick or treating.

But Auntie Peastew

Took me anyway.

Dressed me up

Like a hobo.

With a little ‘fro and makeup

And took me on.

Rowhouse to rowhouse.

Walkup to walkup.

Door to door.

Of Madden Park

Homes.

We had to go.

And when Momma

Came home

From school,

I wished I had better news.

But

I didn’t.

I told her

What happened.

And she said,

“Better had fun,

Cause it’s not

Happenin’

Again.”

Halifax

Water started overflowing

From the rim of the tub

To all the rooms.

Someone forgot

To turn it off.

The faucet had become a fountain.

"Madea, the tub is overflowing

Really bad!"

"Did someone turn it off?"

"No."

Then I don't care if it runs

to Halifax and back.

The Cottage Grove Bus

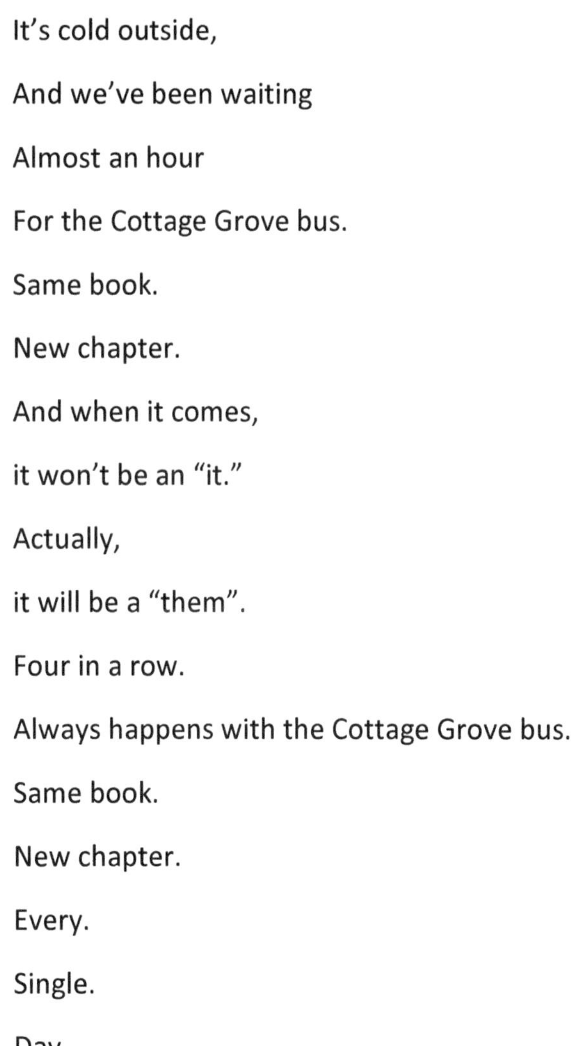

It's cold outside,

And we've been waiting

Almost an hour

For the Cottage Grove bus.

Same book.

New chapter.

And when it comes,

it won't be an "it."

Actually,

it will be a "them".

Four in a row.

Always happens with the Cottage Grove bus.

Same book.

New chapter.

Every.

Single.

Day.

Black repast, baby

Hey baby, I ain't

Seen you in

So long.

So glad to see you, baby.

Have they started putting the food out yet,

Baby?

"Not yet."

I'm ready for some fried chicken.

And potato salad.

I'm tired and hungry.

Funeral and burial

Den wo'

Me out, baby.

My Crown from the King

I love French braiding my hair. *what I don't like is when*

my fingernails

Get caught in my hair.

Pulling and snagging along the way.

But I'm gonna go ahead and make these

Cornrows.

And put my shadow on.

And my hoops.

Wear my queen look.

And walk that walk.

And Talk that talk

of queens.

And Wear my crown

from the King.

The king of glory.

Wading in the Water

I’ve been wading in the water
Too long.
The water of oppression.
And depression.
And dejection.
And regression too long.
I need to get out of the water.
The water the old folks sang about
back in the day.

I’ve been wading in the water
Too long.

The black funeral

Marching, walking, dancing,

Singing.

Tambourine playing.

Preacher beaming.

The black funeral.

Sitting Five hours.

Sweating like showers.

Praying and praying.

Until you're forced to cower.

The black funeral.

Humming and moaning.

Spiritual atoning.

Wailing in circles.

Not a dress rehearsal.

The black funeral.

Do you like it?

Do you like it,
When they ask you
If your hair
Is real?
And they comment
About how much
It has grown.
When yesterday your hair was four
Inches.
And today it is twenty-four
Inches long?
How do you respond
to the questions of why
you wear
Extensions or wigs
That flow down
From the sky?
Do you like it?

It Happened on the Gallery

We used to buy

Those ropes.

And we'd jump

Off and on and in and on

Till we couldn't move

Our legs any more.

This all happened

on the "Gallery".

Matter of fact,

Some of everything happened

On the Gallery.

I bet you didn't know that.

Singing the Bad Songs

Sometimes there were

Groups of teenage boys.

Standing in the hallway

In the projects.

Singing the bad songs.

We knew they were bad.

They had the word diarrhea in them.

But we liked to stand close by.

And listen.

Listen to the beat.

The African beat.

That they made with their hands.

Making the bad songs

Sound like the good songs.

Sometimes there were

Groups of teenage boys.

Standing in the hallway

In the projects.

Singing the bad songs.

The ones with the African beat.

Go to the Sto'

I need you

to go to the sto'.

For me.

Now don't take all day

Long.

Otherwise, I can go myself.

Brush your teeth.

Wash your face.

And go on.

No time for primping.

You can do all that

When you get back.

Bathroom Beauty School

At ten

I did

Not have a clue

As to what

I was doing.

Piling into that tight project

Bathroom,

watching one black

Girl after the next,

French braiding and twisting

Her hair.

Overhand and underhand.

Then underhand and overhand.

Then when I went home,

To the apartment

My momma and I shared.

I would look into

that oval-shaped mirror.

And practice flat-twisting, and French braiding my hair.

Became a pro

At ten.

The things you

Learn

In the

Projects.

The things you

Learn

In the project

Bathrooms.

The skills

You keep

For life.

The Quest

The blacks are forming

A line.

Running

Straight outside

The meat market.

They been building up hope 'cause of

Reading 'bout Sonny boy in *The Defender.*

They hoping to hit the jackpot.

To strike it rich.

To gain a better life for themselves.

Though the quest for a better life led to

A series of traumatic events for me.

A Peppermint Pickle

Ever had a peppermint pickle?
Tastes so good it will leave you feeling fickle.
You have to buy a sour pickle.
Then stick the long, wide peppermint stick in the
middle.
Then you bite a little peppermint.
And then you bite a little pickle.
So cool and so sour,
Got you playing high
on the fiddle.
Have you ever
Had a sweet and sour,
Filled with power
peppermint pickle?

Rubbing and Massaging Their Skin

All the black folks
know about the Vaseline.
It's the one thing we can't do without.
Goes on
Elbows, lips, face, hair.
All over the body.
And those heels if you dare.

When you see black folks with
Vaseline,
Never ask what they gonna do
With it.
It's multipurpose.
A must.
Passed down from generation to generation.
I overdid it when my kids were little.
Peastew said I had their faces shining like
Grease monkeys.

Thought it was okay
Till I saw pictures of their shining
Faces.
Wearing that Vaseline so proudly.
My kids, leaning 'gainst their
Wooden rocking horses.

Hoping one day they
Can pass down the rules
To their kids,
The stories of how the
Black mommas piled it on.

Rubbing and massaging their
Skin.
And kissing the bottoms of the babies.

Then
Rubbing and massaging their
Skin.
And kissing the bumps and the bruises.

Then
Rubbing and massaging their
Skin.
And kissing their teenage heartbreaks away.

Then
Rubbing and massaging their
Skin.
And giving their hands in marriage.

Then
Rubbing and Massaging their
Skin
And watching their grandbabies
Comin' into the world.

And rubbing and massaging their skin
And kissing their bottoms.

When Black Folks Cook

When black folks cook,

They say sit down.

When black folks cook,

They say “stay a while.

Come on over here and

Get you some food.”

When black folks cook,

They say “glad you here.”

When black folks cook,

They say love.

Free As a Bird

I got a bowl of cereal.
Getting ready to watch
Soul Train.
Where the dancers are
free as a bird.
Trying out new moves.
Where the dancers are
free as a bird.
Dressing like a million bucks.
Where the dancers are
free as a bird.
Wearing the stacks and bell bottoms.
Where the dancers are
free as a bird.

Black Folk Dancin'

Dancing makes black folks feel free.
Get the trauma out of their
Bodies.
Get the grief out of their souls.
Make the humming come out of their mouths.
And the spirituals we behold.
You
Start off dancing.
Then end up singing.
And hollerin' and praising the Lord.
Your soul is free as a bird.
Just you and the Lawd.
And the church said Amen.

Caught UP

I made rows and rows of
Cornrows in my hair.
I kind of got caught up
In my artistic flair.

When you're healing

When you're healing,
And you're back to yourself,
You know it.
Less assimilating.
More integrating.
More blackness pushing through.

When you're healing,
And you're back to yourself,
The whole world will know it too.

When I Was a Kid

When I was a kid,
All the black folks
Bought their kids ceramic
Pig banks.
My mother and I
Were on a roll.
Saving our coins.
Hoping to use it for a rainy day.

Then one day,
Our savings ended.
Our pig was stolen.
We were offended.

When I was a kid,
All the black folks
Bought their kids ceramic
Pig banks.

Sang, Baby

Whenever the children’s choir
sang in the big church,
It was a great experience.
All the ladies on the Mother’s board,
And all the missionaries
Waived their handkerchiefs.
And their hats.

‘Sayin’
Sang, baby!
Sang
For the Lawd.”

And we did.
We sang our hearts out.
Till folks were shouting’
And falling’ out.

It is Well

The choir is singing and swaying.
Back and forth.
Fully robed.
Sweating.
Shouting.
Thirty minutes now.
been singing
"It is well"
Till it got a hold of their souls.

Black folks don't cut their little girls' hair

Black folks don't
Cut
Their little girls'
Hair.
No one-year-old.
Two-year-old.
Three-year-old
Haircut.
Afraid of stunting the growth.

They let the glory stay in. To some, doesn't sound like a win. But it is.

It's a generational thing.

And it's drilled in so hard,

That the grandbabies will sing:

"Black folks don't
Cut
Their little girls'
Hair."

Their Feet Are So Wide

Wanna know why
Madea's feet are so wide?
From walking barefoot
Day after day.
running free.
in the fields of the South.
No,
She wasn't physically free.
She was in the Caste.
That's what they called it.

But her soul was free.
Day after day running free.
Her soul ran free
down the streets of gold
In her mind.

And the souls of her ancestors ran free.
That's how they made in the South.
That's why their feet are so wide.

Another Black Person's Funeral

To attend a black person's funeral,
Is to block out five hours of sitting time.
Then two hours of talking time.
Then two hours of burial time.
Then five hours of repast time.
Then a week of recovery time.
To attend a black person's funeral,
Is to venture into the unknown.
Yet, come out on the other side.
As a new man or woman,
Girl or boy.
Ready to celebrate,
And attend,
another black person's funeral.

The Greatest Common Factor

When a child enters school
They learn that the
GCF, or greatest common factor,
Is what their future hinges upon.
As a black person,
Living in society,
They learn that the GCF,
or greatest common factor
is what their future hinges upon.
What is that factor for the black child?
The melanin in your skin
Trumps everything in society.
No amount of wealth, education, beauty, or wisdom
Can ever exceed that fact.
That GCF.
They keep it hidden from the black child.
When the black child can
Allow this truth to seek in,
Their future is bright.
And they can navigate the streets,
The education system.
The professional system.
And sadly,
The church system.
For even the brothers and
Sisters in Christ.
Have kept this factor
A secret.
But knowing how to navigate the GCF
Is what our future hinges upon.

That Black Girl

That black girl.
She didn't make it.
Taken away by society.
Who didn't value her
Or her momma.
Who rubbed her body
Down in Vaseline
Before she left out the door.
She lost her life
To a traffic stop.
The blacks are hurting.
They hurt because
They all feel that it was their daughter.
Their baby.
Their Naa Naa.
Their daughter with blue-black skin
And locks in her long, flowing hair.
And navigating the high school world
As she danced, and twirled, and pop-locked.
And kissed her daddy goodnight at home.
That black girl.
Momma's baby girl
Is gone.
And no explanation in the world can bring her back.
But she runs in the arms of her Savior,
He welcomes her home.
But society didn't welcome her.

That Black Boy

That black boy,
Whose dad showed him the ropes.
But that boy made one wrong
Move.

He decided to answer his phone.
That one decision.
Meant that the po po's
Thought he should be gone.

He was that black boy.
That ashy boy.
Is what his momma called him.
When they were at home in
Their secret haven.
And he hadn't moisturized his body.
And his elbows and heels were screaming for help.

That black boy,
Whose twisties were now
Long and flowing.
HE was hoping to go to
Morehouse.
Learn how to navigate his life as a
Black man.

That black boy.
That teenage boy is gone.
And now his Mom and
Dad are wondering,

Where in the world did
We go wrong?

Underprivileged

They say
That black folks
Just want
To be on welfare.
They are people with
Undeveloped thinking.
In every place.
But the problem
With most
Blacks is that
They are
Constantly
Put back in their place.
I'm ready to graduate.
No, you have ten more classes to take, sir.
I'm ready for a pay raise.
No, you missed two sick days last year, mam.
I'm ready for vacation.
No, so many people have already taken off.
They say that black
Folks
Just want to
Be on welfare.
But the problem
With most
Black folks is that
They are
Constantly
Being Put back in their place.

Pool Hall, Cool Hall

The guys
At the pool hall
Have their bodies situated
Like they are waiting
To take a Sugar Shack photo.
They are leaning in with their arms and elbows
At every kind of angle.
Tipping and nodding their heads
That are wearing those Kangols like a
Hat rack.
And as they are nodding,
They are saying
To the other players
"It's your turn bro'.
Show your blackness.
Show your skill.
Not with fakeness
Taking pills.
Play this game, bro.
Do your best.
Cause this game here.
Is just a test.
A test of the will
And grit.
And endurance.
For the black man,
Carrying his cigar.
In his satchel.
His pouch.
What pouch?

The black folk pouch.
Been 'round since I was a kid.
That royal purple-
Golden-stitched
Crown Royal bag.
The bag that black folks
Used as their multi-purpose
Bag.
The bag that they use
To carry
Their entire life in.
That royal purple-
Golden-stitched
Crown Royal bag.

Brass Clips

I have the gold beads of brass clips in my hair.
Auntie did my hair
Just like this.
I'm marching through the projects.
Looking just like my ancestors did
When they lived in the Motherland.
Each brass clip was carefully placed
Around each flowing braid.
I, Tina, representing the Motherland.

Playing Basketball

I'm playing basketball

With the brothers in my neighborhood.

We're shooting in the yard.

We're dribbling.

We're tooting.

And scribbling on the court.

It's a make-shift setup,

Of milk crates and spray paint.

But, I don't care.

I'm playing basketball

With the brothers in my neighborhood.

And we're bonding just

Like glue in our brotherhood.

Reading While Black

What happens

when you're reading while black?

Reading while black

Leads to assumptions that you

Proper, and then articulate.

Maybe someday you'll be an author.

What happens

when you're reading while black?

Reading while black

Leads to assumptions that you're

Studious, a teacher, a go-getter,

Maybe someday you'll be a preacher.

What happens

when you're reading while black?

Reading while black

Leads to assumptions that you're

Somewhere, that you're dreaming,

That you busting in the seaming.

What happens

when you’re reading while black?

Reading while black means you’re going places

In larger spaces,

Where only God can tie your laces.

What happens

when you’re reading while black?

On a Saturday Night

momma and I
sit up late
rolling and oiling each
other's hair on a Saturday night.
making sure that we're
planting those perfect parts.
sliding a little bit of oil
Down each part with the tip
of the fingers.
cause you know that Royal Crown
hair grease
or the Blue Magic
Is gonna put the finishing touch on that hair.
'cause when momma and I
are done, we'll move on to the manicures,
we got too many
choices of fingernail polish.
hundreds of bottles
lined up on the dresser,
just another layer of

girls’ night bonding,
buffing our nails,
filing, and polishing,
and shining, and dining.
so many moments of
closeness.
when momma and I sit up
late
on a Saturday
night.
rolling and oiling each other’s
hair.

Black Jesus

All the black folks

Have pictures of

Black Jesus

On their walls,

As part of their

Furniture

Décor.

Maybe a China cabinet.

And a few woodknots.

As Madea called them.

And the two TVs

Sitting in

The living room.

One that has sound.

And one that has picture. But,

All the black folks

Have pictures of

Black Jesus

On their walls,

As part of their

Furniture Décor.

Shampooing My Hair

Grandma loved

Shampooing

My hair as a baby.

Massaging my scalp.

Running her fingers

Through my hair.

Putting Creamy Baby Oil in

My scalp.

till

My ringlets looked

Like I had been to

The Beauty Shop and

Given a roller set.

My ringlets are shining.

And my body is smelling good.

Grandma loved

Shampooing

My hair as a baby.

Shirley Temple Curls

I got my Shirley Temple curls.

Dangling and bouncing up and down.

Doesn't happen

Very often.

Kindergarten, Easter, and

A few special occasions.

Madea makes us feel

Special.

When we've got our

Shirley Temple

Curls.

The black Shirley Temple

Curls, that is.

Street Clothes

You know the rules,

When you come in from outside.

You better not

Get on the bed

With your

Street clothes

On.

And you better not let your

Friends do it either.

Visitors Again

Today is the day

That the folks from down-South

Are visiting.

Madea has us washing walls.

And scrubbing cabinet doors

Where the grease from frying chicken

And fish

Took over.

Scrubbing the floors where the many footsteps

Came through.

And Scrubbing the counters where the many roaches camped out.

Today is the day

That the folks from down-South

Are visiting.

French-braiding Momma's Hair

My mother loves it

When I French braid her hair.

Well,

I need to specify.

She doesn't

Like the process.

She likes the result.

The polished look.

Not the pulling

Her brains

Out.

or the headaches.

The result of coworkers

And everybody

And their momma

Complimenting her

On the Cottage Grove bus

On the way home.

My mother loves it

When I French braid her hair.

But, she doesn’t

Like the process.

Everything feels right.

In the summertime

Everybody and their

Momma are out. Kids are playing

In the hydrant water.

It's hot. Stevie

Wonder's playing on the boom

Box.

Everything feels right,

Though it's a lot of wrong

In the world.

Thought it's a lot of drama

Going on in the home.

Being put in our

Place in the caste system

of the workplace.

Doors closed in our

Face.

But we sing and we dance.

Everything feels right,

Though it's a lot of wrong

In the world.

Thought it's a lot of drama

Going on in the home.

Until we as a people

Get home

With Jesus

Then everything

Will be right.

Till then, we sing, and we dance.

Cause Everything feels right.

Though it's a lot of wrong going on

In the world.

Sister Henderson

Getting my praise on at church.

So, I thought.

Till Sister Henderson

Said she's going to tell

Momma.

Cause she caught me

Talking to

Mother Wilson's

Grandson over in the prayer room.

When word gets out, I

Know that I'm done.

Till then,

I will keep

Getting my praise on at church.

Hoping that I see Johnny,

Mother Wilson's grandson.

Digging deep down in those roots

Digging deep down in those roots

But what does

That mean?

Going to the beginning

The moment of sinning

When our nation did its thing.

Digging deep down in those roots

But what does

That mean?

Knowing The paths

that you are walking.

And the language

you are talking.

Will not define your

Your entire being.

Digging deep down in those roots

But what does

That mean?

Savoring the gifts

you've been given

Knowing that life is

Worth livin'

And letting it sink into your seams.

Digging deep down in those roots

But what does

That mean?

Walking and wailing

Till grief has taken over.

Linking with black arms, and

Black heads,

And black shoulders.

Standing so strong.

When you know you've been wronged.

Praying with our people

Way To God's Holy steeple.

Praying so long,

With our 400-year song.

Digging and digging,

Till there’s no more reneging,

And..

you’re digging deep down in those roots.

Acknowledgments

To God be the glory for giving me the strength and opportunity to write for him once again.

This book would not have possible without hearing the stories of my grandmother, mother, aunts, and cousins, paving the way for their descendants to dig deep down in their roots.

And let the church say, *Amen*.

Check out the

"The Valley of Grace Podcast"

on iTunes, Spotify, Stitcher, Castos, Google and Apple Podcast, & YouTube

For more books by Katina Horton, head over to Amazon, Barnes & Nobles, and your local bookstore to request the following titles:

Do not forget to kindly leave a review!

ABOUT THE AUTHOR

Katina Horton is a life coach, author, speaker, podcaster, computer technician, and the mother of two young-adult children.

Her podcast, THE VALLEY OF GRACE PODCAST, focuses on helping women create an empowered new chapter of life in every area.

As a coach, she uses the core concepts of trouble-shooting your PC, building a PC, and creating new software to help women in difficult relationships break unhealthy relationship cycles, reclaim their power and identity, build resilience and flourish, and in turn, create an empowered new chapter of life for themselves.

She has written nine books, including The Journey, Surrendered, Simply Grace, Valley of Grace, Coming Out of the Valley, Broken Pieces, A Survivor's Point of View, My Blackness & DIGGING DEEP DOWN IN THOSE ROOTS.

Through speaking, she motivates women using spiritual and spoken word poetry, along with a unique and engaging storytelling style that inspires, motivates, empowers, and impacts the audiences for generations to come.

For more information on Katina Horton, or to schedule a speaking event, go to https://thevalleyofgrace.com.

www.ingramcontent.com/pod-product-compliance
Lightning Source LLC
Chambersburg PA
CBHW070550310726
48982CB00011B/1530/J

* 9 7 8 0 5 7 8 9 2 0 5 9 7 *